Trevor Harvey

Operation
Pedal Paw

Illustrated by Jane Gedye

YOUNG
LIONS

First published in Great Britain in Young Lions 1991

Young Lions is an imprint of the Children's Division,
part of HarperCollins Publishers Ltd,
77–85 Fulham Palace Road, Hammersmith,
London W6 8JB

Copyright © Trevor Harvey 1991

Illustrations copyright © Jane Gedye 1991

ISBN 0 00 673802–8

Set in Garamond
Printed and bound in Great Britain by
HarperCollins Manufacturing, Glasgow

I

It all starts when our teacher, Miss Harris, decides it was time for "metamorphosis". That means you've turned into something else when you wake up the morning after you've watched a Late Night Horror film, like *Dracula Meets Our Dental Surgeon*.

"You're just lying in bed," Miss Harris begins, "and you feel different . . ."

"That's because it's a flower bed," mutters Warren.

Sandra thumps him over the head with her dictionary.

"Stop that, Sandra!" sighs Miss Harris. "Books cost money."

"Sorry, miss," Sandra simpers, in a sickly voice that always manages to fool teachers.

It works again. Miss Harris smiles and her teeth shine pearly-white. Yuck.

"How will you move about?" she continues. "What can you wear? What do you eat?" She is getting really excited about *her* idea for *our* story.

"What new enemies will you find? What do you do when you reach school?"

"The usual old rubbish," Warren mutters again.

I like Warren. He's on my wavelength.

He's also at the next desk.

This time Miss *must* have heard – but she pretends she hasn't, and she starts writing on the blackboard. Squeak.

"Use your rough books to work out the ideas. Here is your title: THE DAY I TURNED INTO A. . . I want neat handwriting and good spelling. Whatever you do, don't forget your punctuation. Put the date on the right-hand side, then miss a line. Underline the title. Make sure you leave a margin. Don't cross out. Don't blot out. Don't rub out."

Don't peg out.

Honestly, she's been like this ever since they introduced the National Curriculum. It's a wonder we get anything written at all, with all the stuff she expects us to remember.

Five minutes later Warren stops writing. I lean over to look at what he's written. It turns out he has changed into a slug and he gets squashed on the third line.

"Finished already, Warren?"

"Yes, miss."

HEADMISTRESS
MRS BRANDON

"Bring me your book, please."

Pretty soon Warren is back in his seat. He sighs and picks up his pen. He's got to think about reincarnating himself.

Then she starts staring at me.

"How about you, Andrew? Have you finished, too?"

"Yes, miss."

"Bring it here, boy."

I clasp the book in both hands and hug it to my chest, as if to stop the other kids from pinching my ideas as I slouch past them. Miss Harris doesn't seem too impressed when she reads what I've put.

"What's this?" she snaps. "Read your title to the class."

"The Day I turned into a Lay-By," I gulp.

Suddenly I know I'll have to do some quick thinking.

"I was driving along the A1 when I knew I would have to turn into a Lay-By," I begin. The rest of the class giggle.

I think it's pretty witty myself, but Miss Harris hasn't got a sense of humour.

"Go and tell Mrs Brandon!" she shouts. "Go on – at once!"

There are three white cardboard boxes outside the head's room. One has been placed on top of another, with the third box at their side. Two have the words COMPUTER – WITH CARE written in large red letters. The other box has WORD PROCESSOR – WITH CARE written in large black letters. I know what that means. More stories for Miss Harris. She's hoping we'll be desk-top publishers instead of desk-top graffiti carvers.

The door of the head's office is half open and I can see that she's sitting at her desk and she's busy writing – perhaps a teacher has asked *her* to have a go at a story, too?

I cough – but very very quietly. It seems a shame to interrupt her.

I wait for a while, and then decide that the best thing to do is tiptoe away.

"*Yes*, Andrew . . . ?" booms Mrs Brandon, almost giving me a heart attack. So, she *has* heard me after all!

"I – I wanted to see you," I reply.

"Well, why don't you knock so I know you're there?" she says.

Our head teacher is as batty as the rest of them. One minute she's talking to me, and the next minute she's telling me to knock so she knows I'm there.

I don't argue. I've given up trying to work out what goes on in the heads of these adults. I do as I'm told and I knock at her door.

"Who is it?" she asks.

For a moment, my mind goes blank.

"Ah, Andrew," she says. "What can I do for you?"

"I've turned into a Lay-By," I reply.

I can see the dots in her eyes getting smaller.

"What?" she asks.

"I've turned into a Lay-By. Miss Harris told me to tell you."

"Miss Harris did?"

"Yes."

She leans back in her chair and taps her fingers together, thoughtful-like.

"Well," she says, "let's hope it's an improvement."

I stand sheepishly and clutch at my closed book.

"Is there anything else?" she enquires.

I shake my head.

"Then what are you waiting for? Back to your classroom, Andrew." She looks down at her desk and starts writing again. I breathe a sigh of relief.

I decide not to hurry back. Well, I've only been gone a minute or two – hardly time for all the drama Miss Harris is expecting.

Just before the bell is due to ring for morning break, I wander back to the classroom with my head bowed.

"Well . . . ?" Miss Harris asks. "Did you see the head?"

"Yes," I whisper.

"I expect she said something about *improvement*."

"Yes," I answer.

I am amazed by her powers. Honestly, these teachers – I begin to wonder whether they're psychic or something?

During break, Sandra comes up to me and says, "I bet you *didn't* go to see the head, Marshy Mellows!"

"Bet I did!" I reply and glare at her, saying a magic spell inside my head to turn her into a disgusting-looking warthog. It doesn't work. I'll have to practise more.

As we're going back in after break, I feel a hand on my shoulder. I'm just about to turn round to give Warren a friendly swipe when a voice says, "Andrew, I think you and I need to have a little chat . . ."

"You're to stay in my study for the rest of the morning," Mrs Brandon says. I think of all the work I'll be missing with Miss Harris, but I manage to stop myself from smiling just in time. Well, I don't want Mrs Brandon to get the idea I'm not worried – otherwise she might send me back to class straightaway.

She sits me in the corner of the room and tells me to start my story "all over again".

"And we don't want any more Lay-Bys, do we?" she says.

I suck the end of my pen and act like I'm

11

thinking.

I must be good at it because it's a whole five minutes before she tells me to get on with my work.

Almost as soon as I start writing, there's a knock at the door and Mrs Potts (she's the school secretary) appears. She's got her white beads on today, so that means she's in a bad mood.

"A policeman wants a word with you, Mrs Brandon!" she snaps. I glance at the head but she doesn't look worried. Perhaps someone has complained about the school cook at last. We all know she's been trying to poison everyone for *years*! Her spotted dick is bad enough but her mutton curries are deadly!

Anyway, by now my ears are well and truly ready to record every word of the conversation. A burly police sergeant enters the room. I have to confess, this surprises me. I *had* been expecting to see Constable Williams – he's the School's Liaison Officer. When Constable Williams comes to talk to a class, he tells you things like which end of his police dog bites and he puts handcuffs on someone, then pretends that he's lost the key.

"Oh dear!" he says. "You'll have to stay like that all day . . ."

The first time he tried it, he put them on Miss

Harris and he said he'd have to take her away with him down to the station and could we manage without her. Everyone screamed "YES!" – so he found the key straightaway and unlocked her – which was a big disappointment, really. Still, his talk *did* get us out of having to do maths that day. We had to write a newspaper report of his visit instead. I made up a good headline: POLICE DOG SAVAGES TEACHER. LITTLE HOPE AS SUSPECTED LEADER OF THE MAFIA LIES IN INTENSIVE CARE. I got sent to Mrs Brandon that day as well.

I lean back too far on my chair and it topples over with a crash, sending me sprawling. The police sergeant turns and glares at me and Mrs Brandon remembers that I'm there.

"Run along," she says, "and work for a while

in Mrs Potts's office."

I curse the chair for toppling over. Now I may never know why a police sergeant is visiting our school.

I come out of the head's office and do a slight detour to look again at the boxes. The one containing the word processor is open, so I pull back the flap and begin to poke about among the shavings.

"What are you doing? Why are you out of your classroom?"

Mrs Potts has either had closed circuit cameras set up in the corridor or else she can see through walls. I enter the secretary's office and explain that Mrs Brandon has sent me.

Mrs Potts glares at me over her typewriter.

"Sit still and touch *nothing* – understand?"

I look round the room. I can't see anything that's worth touching, so I nod my head.

Mrs Potts attacks the typewriter keys as if she is thumping out a death threat. She doesn't need a poison pen, I'm sure she's got a poison typewriter ribbon. I open my book and write as I have never written before.

After a while, there are voices in the corridor.

"Don't let the children worry too much," says the police sergeant to Mrs Brandon, as they pause for a moment outside the open door of the

Secretary's office. "Just tell them to be on their guard. We don't want any more bicycles stolen."

"No," answers Mrs Brandon. "And we'll certainly keep an eye open for those rabbit thieves."

Then the sergeant leaves and Mrs Brandon comes into the office. Perhaps I'll hear the whole story now . . .

But instead, Mrs Brandon's looking at me.

"Andrew – let's see how your story is progressing, shall we?" She takes the book and I watch her as she begins to read.

"Ah," she says. "Yes – very interesting. . . ."

By the time you reach Year Five you know that when teachers say something is "very interesting" they really mean it's not much good but you've tried hard so they don't want to put you off.

"There!" she says, quickly handing me the book back. "I knew you'd be able to think of *something*." I have. I've called my story THE DAY I TURNED INTO A WARTHOG. "Now – back to your class. It's almost lunchtime."

I hurry to the room, armed not only with my story for Miss Harris but also with information about cops and robbers, bicycles and rabbits – information that no one else in the school knows. This lunchtime, I shall be the person *everyone* wants to talk to.

II

"You're just making it up, Marshy Mellows!"

I wish Sandra wouldn't keep calling me that. I'd like to give her a thump but everyone knows she's the best fighter in the school. You don't mix it with Sandra.

I pretend I don't hear her comments on my story, but Warren's reaction comes as a bit of a blow.

"I don't get it!" he says.

"I'm just telling you what I heard."

"But *rabbits* stealing *bicycles* – it doesn't make sense! I mean, how would their paws reach the pedals?"

I have to confess, Warren's got a point there.

"And how would they keep their balance?" chips in Sandra, who's still hanging around.

I think fast again – that's the second time in one day.

"Of course, they don't have to be *real* rabbits . . ." I tell them.

"What – you mean, they could be tortoises or

16

gerbils?" suggests Warren.

"No!" I reply, still thinking furiously. "They could – they could be *humans* in rabbit costumes . . ."

"I see — stealing bicycles to get rabbits a bad name? Perhaps they crouch down low to disguise their size?"

"You're nuts, Warren Henton!" sneers Sandra. "And you're a liar, Marshy Mellows! You ought to be back in the Infants!"

"You wait," I call out to Sandra as she moves away, "when Mrs Brandon tells the whole school, we'll see if I'm a liar then!"

But Mrs Brandon doesn't tell the whole school. I wait all afternoon for her to call a special assembly – but she doesn't even send a note round for the teachers to read.

"Some story!" sneers Sandra, as the bell rings for home time.

"Some rabbits!" sighs Warren.

I make my way across the playground towards the sheds, deep in thought. Could I have misheard? Could it all have been a dream? That's the way Timothy Phillips usually finishes *his* stories, when he can't think what to write. Miss Harris doesn't get annoyed with him, though. He's the teacher's pet, that's why. Timothy Phillips – he's even got the right initials.

I reach the sheds – and stop still in amazement.

I look this way and that.

I search high and low – but it isn't there.

Those rabbits must have struck again.

My bicycle has disappeared . . .

At first, I wonder whether Warren has played a trick on me and hidden my bike somewhere. But then I remember that Warren's mum called for him at home time to take him to the dentist.

So I realize it's no joke. My bike has well and truly gone.

I rush into school (which is something I wouldn't usually do) and I scream at the top of my voice as I run.

"RABBITS!"

Mr Higgs, the caretaker, glares at me as he rests his hands on the top of his broom handle.

"None of that language here," he snaps. I gallop down the corridor towards the head's study.

"HEY!" Mr Higgs shouts after me.

I turn my head to see what he wants.

"Watch where you're going!" he says.

Unfortunately, his warning comes a bit late. There is a sudden, sickening impact. It feels as though I've made contact with a centurion tank.

It turns out to be Mrs Potts, who has come out of her office and is standing directly in my path. Or was standing.

Mrs Potts lets out a hideous scream.

Looking back, I see that I have knocked her over. She is staring up at the ceiling, waving her arms and legs in the air and clutching at her throat.

Lots of little white things go rolling by.

For a moment, I think I've knocked her teeth out . . .

When I look again, they seem a bit too round.

"My pearls!" she screams. "My lovely pearls!"

Mr Higgs drops his broom and comes running, holding out a hand to help Mrs Potts up.

Suddenly, there is a CRUNCH.

He's managed to find one of the beads.

"CAREFUL, MR HIGGS! You're clod-hopping all over my pearls!"

Mrs Potts takes a firm hold of Mr Higgs's outstretched hand – but somehow she manages to catch him off balance and he crashes down on top of her.

More beads start rolling free and, by this time, the head appears at her study door.

"What on earth's going on?" she asks, staring down at the crumpled forms of Mrs Potts and Mr Higgs.

"Rabbits!" I cry, still breathless from my running.

"What?" asks the head as Mrs Potts and Mr

Higgs scramble to their feet.

There is another crunch.

This time, Mrs Potts's left shoe has found one of her beads.

"Quick – everybody down on their knees!" wails Mrs Potts as she starts searching behind the cardboard box labelled COMPUTER – WITH CARE. Mrs Brandon watches her, still bewildered.

"I'll ask again," Mrs Brandon says – and I can tell by her voice that she is trying to keep as calm as possible. 'What *is* happening?"

"Ask *him*!" snarls Mrs Potts – and she points at me. I notice her face is now as white as her beads.

'Well . . . ?" enquires Mrs Brandon.

"Rabbits . . ." I say, meekly.

"That boy should be banned from the school!" Mrs Potts mutters as she crawls around the floor searching for the missing millions.

"Come into my study, Andrew." The head doesn't look too happy, so I rise to my feet and do as I'm told.

There's another *crunch*. My right foot has made contact with a bead. At this rate, Mrs Potts should have at least one less row to worry about in future.

"Careful!" she snarls. I notice that the colour is slowly returning to her cheeks.

21

As I reach the head's door, there is one further *crunch*.

It's the head this time. Well, it's only fair that we should all have a go, isn't it?

"Sorry, Mrs Potts," she says.

Mrs Potts says nothing, but by now her face resembles an over-ripe tomato.

"Now then, Andrew – what's this about?" Mrs Brandon asks me as soon as we are alone in her study.

Somehow I blurt it all out – about the bicycles and the rabbits and the police sergeant and no special assembly.

"Not even a note to the teachers!" I add, accusingly.

Mrs Brandon sinks slowly on to her chair.

"Sit down, Andrew," she says. "You and I must have another little chat . . ."

I've heard adults say things like that before – so I know what's coming. I'm going to be told not to be silly and to "act my age". But, as it happens, that's *not* what Mrs Brandon says.

She tells me that the police sergeant came round because he's just been moved to the area and he wants his daughter to join our school. It seems only one bike has been stolen in the area and five rabbits have gone missing from a local infant

school.

I still like my story better, so I decide to stick to it.

Besides, *two* bikes are missing now, not one.

Mrs Potts is just getting up from her knees as

Mrs Brandon opens her study door and walks with me along the corridor.

"I'll check the bicycle shed with you," the head decides, "in case your bike has been returned."

She does – but nothing's there.

Mrs Brandon frowns and then asks me details about its make and what it looks like.

"I'll make out a report for you to the police. I expect they may wish to call and see you." She puts an arm round my shoulders. "Don't worry, Andrew. I'm sure it will turn up soon."

Some hope! I think – but I smile weakly at her because I know she's only trying to be helpful.

"Oh – before you go . . . You didn't *really* think there were rabbits riding around on bicycles, did you?"

"No, miss," I answer, with my fingers crossed behind my back.

III

Friday night is difficult. Mum *and* Dad keep making remarks about bikes not growing on trees.

Next morning is Saturday, and Mum seems more friendly again.

"Do you think you could have left it somewhere?" she says.

"What?" I ask, through a mouthful of Corn Flakes.

"Your bike. Do you think you've mislaid it? Taken it to your auntie's or lent it to a friend and forgotten about it?"

I decide there's nothing for it – I'll have to find who stole the bike and prove to my parents they've got a son who's not as daft as they think. Trouble is – where to start?

I call round at Warren's house, but he's not up yet.

The dentist hasn't finished his work and Warren's got to see him that morning for a couple of fillings.

"Passed right out, he did," says Warren's mum.

"Who – the dentist?" I ask.

"No! *Warren*," she says. "As soon as he saw the dentist's drill. I told him to look up at the Mickey Mouse mobile – but would he? Not him! He never listens to a thing I say. And then, when he came round, he refused to open his mouth – so the dentist said he'd try again today. That means I've got to make another journey with him, as if I hadn't enough to do already!"

I get an idea.

"If you like, Mrs Henton, *I'll* go the dentist with Warren . . ."

"What's that, love?"

"I said *I'll* take Warren to the dentist."

She beams at me. "Oh, *would* you, Andrew? That'd be such a help. You don't know just how helpful!" She goes to her purse and gives me a pound. "He won't go on his own – he's such a baby for someone his age."

My hand's still open, so she makes it two pounds.

Mrs Henton shouts upstairs: "WARREN! Warren, do you hear me? You've got a visitor."

Warren's voice drifts feebly down: "If it's the dentist, tell him I'm staying here."

"It's your friend – Andrew. Now, you just get up and come down, smartish!"

After a few minutes, Warren clumps down the stairs, looking like something nasty the dog's brought in.

"Wash your face, comb your hair – and I thought I told you to put that T-shirt with egg mayonnaise all over it into the wash *days* ago."

Warren does as he's told.

We get out of the house as soon as we can.

"Eleven thirty," Mrs Henton calls after me. "Don't forget."

I nod.

"What's she mean, eleven thirty?" Warren asks, as we walk down the road.

I gulp, then say, "I promised I'd take you to the dentist."

"I thought you were my friend," he replies. "You said we were going for a walk."

"We are," I answered. "Listen – terrible things happened after school yesterday!" I give Warren an in-depth account of how the bike went missing, of how the beads and Mrs Potts parted company and of the little chat I had with Mrs Brandon.

"See!" he says. "I told you it couldn't have been rabbits stealing those bikes!" He looks too smug for my liking.

"Yeah – well," I reply, "I still think there's a

connection somehow – and we're going to prove it . . ."

"*We* are?" he asks. His eyes open wide, as if they're a pair of saucers. "How are we going to do that?"

"You've read those Famous Five stories, Warren . . ."

"Yeah, but there's only two of us . . ."

"The Famous Five use their imagination and they never have any trouble. So that's what *we've* got to do."

"OK. Where to, then?"

"What?"

"Where do we start searching for the bike?"

"Oh – back at school, of course," I reply.

"SCHOOL?" shouts Warren. "I'm not going to school, not on a Saturday!" I can see he's not pleased.

"We've got to take a look at the scene of the crime, blockhead," I tell him.

"But we know what school looks like already," says Warren.

"Not when it's empty. We can search the bicycle shed for clues, like real detectives, before everything gets disturbed."

"You won't find tyre tracks if that's what you're looking for," says Warren. "Not on a concrete

surface. You need mud for that." I begin to wonder why I've brought Warren with me. But he is company – and I can't go snooping around the school on my own. I need someone to act as a lookout for Higgs, the caretaker. It would be just my luck to have *him* turning up right in the middle of things.

He does.

As it happens, Warren is not a very good lookout.

"LOOK OUT!" he cries – and I turn round to see Mr Higgs standing right beside me.

I had climbed over the railings by the locked playground gate, leaving Warren outside, peering through. I had crept stealthily across the play-ground to the bicycle shed and taken out the Super Detective magnifying glass which I had just bought with Mrs Henton's pounds at the newsagent's shop on the corner. (It turned out to be cheap plastic – and when I peered through it the image was all blurred.) It was then that Warren gave his warning cry – a bit late. I found out afterwards he'd been busy stroking Florence, the caretaker's cat. She had obviously been sent as a decoy.

"What are you looking for?" asks Mr Higgs – and he adds, sarcastically, "It wouldn't be rabbits by any chance, would it?"

I have to think quickly again.

"No," I reply. "It's woodlice."

"*Woodlice*? Ah, woodlice, is it? Planning to become a naturalist now, are you?" he asks.

"Certainly not," I reply. "People should only take their clothes off when they have a bath."

This seems to satisfy him for his face shows a flicker of a smile.

"It still doesn't explain what you're doing in this playground," he says. "You can find woodlice in your own backyard."

"Not this one," I answer. "It's a pet . . ."

"A pet?" He almost drops his broom. "A *pet*? A pet *woodlouse*?"

"Yes," I reply, meekly.

"You'll be telling me next it's got a name!"

"Russell," I answer. "I keep it in a matchbox in my pocket and it must have escaped yesterday when I was searching for my bike."

Mr Higgs sneers and strokes his chin. "And how do you plan to tell this – Russell – if you find him? What's different about him from other woodlice? I suppose he sings songs or does backward flips?"

"Certainly not," I say and I try to look offended. "He answers to his name, if you must know." I call, "Here, Russell – come here, boy," and peer at the ground through the magnifying glass as I slowly edge my way nearer to those playground railings.

Mr Higgs sees Warren, who's staring in at us, looking as if he's behind bars.

"Oi, you!" he shouts at Warren. "Have you come searching for Russell as well?"

"What?" asks Warren, looking blank.

"Russell, lad – Russell!"

"I don't think I can," he replies and he starts brushing his arms backwards and forwards over his clothes.

I've always thought Warren wasn't too bright.

Higgs watches him in amazement – and this gives me my chance to make a break for it. I'm over

the railings before Higgs knows what's happened.

"Scarper!" I shout to Warren.

"HEY, YOU! COME BACK HERE!" Higgs calls – and I can hear his keys jingling on his key-ring as he searches for the right one to unlock the gate. "You wait until Monday!"

Warren and I don't wait until Monday.

We speed down the road until we're sure Higgs isn't following us, and then collapse against the churchyard wall to get our breath back.

"Why – didn't – you – warn – me – sooner – *blockhead*!" I pant.

It's then Warren tells me about stroking Florence.

It's then we realize that Florence is still in Warren's hands.

"You fool! What did you want to pick her up for?"

Florence is wondering the same thing. She lets out a loud miaow and wriggles free.

"Hang on to her, Warren!" I cry, but it's too late. Florence has scarpered into the churchyard.

"Now you've done it!"

"Weren't my fault."

"We've got to get her back – she'll be lost."

"Rabbits, bicycles – and a bloomin' cat. I think I should have stayed in bed after all . . ."

"Belt up," I tell him, "and help me search for her."

This time there's no need to scramble over a wall, for the church gate's already open – well, it's

off its hinges, anyway.

In the few seconds it takes us to follow Florence into the churchyard, she manages to disappear from sight. I look behind some ancient gravestones to see if she's settled down to wash herself, but no such luck.

"You been in here before?" asks Warren.

"No," I answer. "Have you?"

"'Course not," he replies. "I don't like graveyards – they're spooky."

"Not in broad daylight," I tell him. "Anyway, I thought it was dentists you didn't like?"

I scramble over a couple of concrete slabs and make my way to the rear of the churchyard.

It's then that I see it – but it isn't meant to be seen. Half hidden, among the bushes, against the back wall, is a bike.

IV

For a moment, I forget about Florence.

For a moment, I hope it's *my* bike and it's going to be restored to me. But then I see that it's too large and too old – a man's bike, not a kid's bike, and one that could do with a lick of paint.

"WARREN!" I yell. "Come over here!"

"Have you found her?" he asks.

"No – but you just wait till you see what I *have* found! Quick – search the rest of these bushes! Perhaps there are other bikes hidden here."

Warren and I scramble about, exploring the bushes – but all we come up with is a broken rattle and a well-chewed tennis ball.

"Nothing," sighs Warren.

I don't like being beaten.

"This bike's *something*," I say. "Look at the way it's been hidden. Perhaps – perhaps there are others in parks and churchyards all round the town! Just waiting to be collected . . . when they're *ready* . . ."

"Ready?" says Warren. "Ready for what?"

"To make their move," I reply.

"Oh," says Warren. I'm glad he doesn't ask me *what* move.

By this time, Warren has climbed on to a stone and is standing on tiptoe, looking over the crumbling wall round the churchyard.

"Shall we take the bike to the police station?" I say.

"We'd better, I suppose," Warren answers.

"Come on, then," I reply – but he is still staring over the wall.

"Andrew," he says, slowly. "I think I've found the rabbits . . . I think they're over this wall . . ."

I push Warren off the stone to climb up and have a look for myself. What I see is a wild, over-

grown bit of wasteland, surrounded on the other sides by ancient wooden fencing.

And – Warren's right.

In the centre is a wire cage.

And in the cage are – six white rabbits.

I can see the headlines now:

BOYS RESCUE KIDNAPPED RABBITS.

Or:

BOY DETECTIVES RESCUE KIDNAPPED
RABBITS.

Or better still:

BRAVE BOY DETECTIVES RESCUE
KIDNAPPED RABBITS.

"It's them! Trouble is, there are six of them. Mrs Brandon said only five were missing."

"Perhaps they had one already," suggests Warren.

Something's not right, somehow.

A man's bike rather than a kid's bike.

Six rabbits rather than five.

And yet . . .

And yet it's all too much of a coincidence to ignore it. After all, they've taken more than one bike, so why shouldn't they take more than five rabbits?

"Warren," I say, confidently, "it's time for us to put Operation Pedal Paw into action!"

"Operation what?" he says.

I start wishing that Miss Harris had let Warren remain a squashed slug after all.

Suddenly, we are interrupted by a strange whistling sound.

There's the scrunch of footsteps on the gravel path.

We've got a visitor.

Someone else has entered the churchyard.

I jump off the stone and fling myself at Warren. My hand goes over his mouth to stop him talking.

"HEY!" he yells, and almost bites my fingers off.

The footsteps and whistling stop. Whoever it is has heard Warren and is looking around to see where the shout has come from. But, by this time, I have pulled Warren to the ground. We are both hidden behind a large tombstone.

"Ssshh, you idiot," I whisper in his ear. "Someone's coming! I don't want them to see us. . ."

Warren gets the message and lies as flat as I do. We don't move a muscle.

Suddenly, the footsteps start up again – really slow.

"I said this place was haunted," whispers Warren.

We hold our breath as the footsteps pass within

an arm's length of us, on the other side of the tombstone. Then the sound stops.

After a few seconds I feel brave enough to peer over the top of the stone slab.

"It's a man," I whisper to Warren.

Luckily, the bloke's got his back to me. He's standing right in front of the rusty bicycle, pulling aside the bushes that were half hiding it.

By now, Warren has plucked up courage and he's peering over the top of the tombstone as well.

The man with his back to us is tall and balding. He looks even older than my dad. He is wearing a black overcoat with the collar half turned up, and what looks like a black scarf. He is also wearing bicycle clips round the bottoms of his black trousers.

"They're to stop the rabbits," whispers Warren.

"Rabbits?" I hiss. "What are you on about now?"

"He's wearing cycle clips so the rabbits can't run up his trouser legs," Warren explains.

The trouble is, I think Warren believes it.

We watch as the bike is moved slowly away from the bushes.

"Down!" I hiss – and we duck behind the tombstone again. I can hear the bike being wheeled to the churchyard gate. We make our way behind the

row of tombstones until we reach a spot where we
can see what's happening. We get there just in time
to watch the man grasp the handlebars and climb
on to the bike. He wobbles for a moment, then
gets his balance and rides out of sight.

"What do we do now?" Warren asks.

"Follow him, of course!" I reply.

But that's easier said than done.

By the time we reach the gate, the man has done
a Florence on us. He and the bike are nowhere in
sight.

Florence! I'd forgotten about her. If it weren't
for that cat, we'd never have seen the bicycle – or
the rabbits – or the man in the black clothes.

"Now what?" sighs Warren.

I look at my wristwatch. "Dentist," I say.

"Do me a favour!" Warren replies.

"I am," I answer. "Your teeth will feel like new – and your mum will be so pleased she'll let you go out this afternoon with your go-cart."

"Go-cart?" says Warren, mouth wide open like a fish. "She never lets me out on my own with it."

"You won't be on your own – *I'll* be with you. And she'll know she can trust me, once you've been to the dentist, won't she?"

Warren still seems unsure. "But what do I want a go-cart for? Everywhere's crowded on a Saturday."

"To collect the rabbits, of course – we've got to put them in something, haven't we? Once I've got you home from the dentist, we'll make plans to come back here again this afternoon. OK? We can have a good search for Florence at the same time – it's too late now. Right?" I look at my watch again. "It's exactly eleven twenty-five. If we run, it's down Grindley Hill, 'cross the zebra, past the supermarket and into Welbeck Road – that's the surgery your mum said you go to, isn't it?"

"*Run* to the dentist? You must be joking!" groans Warren – but I give him a kick-start to help him on his way.

V

The appointment was for eleven thirty but Warren has to wait. By the time he's been done, it has taken almost an hour. I'm bored. I've read all the magazines worth looking at long before the receptionist even called Warren's name. When she does, Warren looks green – as if he's about to be sick. I glare at him and tell him that Operation Pedal Paw is relying on him. So off he goes, to open his mouth nice and wide.

Meanwhile, there's nothing to do but sit and wait. I twiddle my thumbs – from clockwise to anti-clockwise, then anti-clockwise to clockwise. I swing my legs back and forth against the chair, until I see the receptionist frowning at me over her glasses.

The door from the street opens and who should walk in but Mrs Potts, the school secretary. She looks different on a Saturday, somehow. She glares at me, then turns away and finds a chair to sit down. We spend the rest of the time pretending not to know each other. I begin to wonder if I did knock any of her teeth out after all. One thing's certain – she's not wearing her beads.

I can't get over the fact that Mrs Potts goes to the same dentist as Warren. "It's a small world," I say out loud.

An old man looks up from his newspaper, coughs and then starts reading again.

"Education!" he mutters. "Waste of money."

After a while, Warren emerges from the surgery, looking even greener than when he went in. He is being supported in the arms of the nurse.

One chap who has been sitting nervously in the corner of the waiting room decides it's time to go home. I can't blame him. Warren looks like one of those government health warnings. He's so ill he doesn't even see Mrs Potts as I hurry outside with him.

"Ugh enno eek," he burbles at me. After he tries it a couple of times, I work out what he's trying to say. His gums still feel numb so he's finding it hard to talk.

"Don't worry," I tell him. "When we get to your house, leave all the talking to me. I'll get your mum to let us take out your go-cart if it's the last thing I do."

It nearly is . . .

We leave the dentist's and climb Grindley Hill.

"Can't – we – catch – a – bus – home?" Warren says, in a blurred sort of way.

"We haven't any money," I reply. "We spent

what your mum gave us on that magnifying glass
– remember?"

We pause for breath at the top of Grindley Hill
and then begin to stroll slowly along in the direction of home. Very soon we're back by the churchyard again, and Warren decides to stop for a
breather.

I wander into the churchyard to look over the
wall and make sure the rabbits are still waiting for
us. They are. And you'll never guess what I see on
this side of the wall – the bike! It's been returned!

Warren seems surprised when I wheel the bike
out.

"What're you doing?" he gawps.

"Keeping it safe," I reply, "until we can find
out who it really belongs to. I'm wheeling it home.
We can put it in your shed."

"You can't do that!" cries Warren. "My mum'll
go nuts!"

"She won't if you don't tell her."

"But you'll get us both done for stealing!"

"It's not stealing, it's minding. We're looking
after it. If you're going to be a private detective,
you've got to take risks."

"But I'm not going to be a private detective. I'm
going to be a bus driver."

That's the trouble with Warren – he's got no

imagination.

When we get near the school, we decide to cross the road just to be on the safe side. We don't want to find that Mr Higgs has been waiting behind the gate for us, ready to pounce out and drag us into the playground.

As it happens, he hasn't – which is all a big disappointment, really. We just about get past when I catch sight of him wandering out through the main school door. He doesn't see us, but he is scratching his head and calling, "Florence – for the last time, are you coming in to have your fish?"

I hope the fish is fresh. It could be in for a long wait.

VI

Warren's garden shed isn't as secluded as I'd hoped.

We go along the dustman's path at the back of his garden, to keep out of sight as best we can, but one of his neighbours is hanging out her washing.

"Where did you find that pile of junk?" she says.

"Oh, this is Andrew, my friend," he answers.

"I'm talking about that bike you're hiding behind your back," she says. "I hope your mum's not going to let you ride up and down our alley all day long."

"No, Mrs Riley," Warren smiles at his neighbour and she turns to peg a tea towel on the line.

We wedge the bike among an array of flowerpots in the garden shed and then I push Warren towards his kitchen door.

"How's your mouth now?" I ask.

"OK," he replies.

"Well, it won't be if you let your mum know what we've been doing. Not a word about the bike

or the rabbits. The dentist just took a long time, remember?"

"You boys are late back," Mrs Henton says as we wipe our shoes on the kitchen mat. "Well?" she asks. "The truth now – *did* you get Warren to the dentist?"

"Cross my heart and hope to die," I say. "You can ask Mrs Potts if you like . . ."

"Mrs Potts?" Warren's mum looks surprised. "What's she got to do with it?"

"It was her that made us late," I lie. "She had to have all her teeth out. It took the dentist hours."

"Oh, the poor woman!" Mrs Henton has gone into a sort of daze. "I must make sure I have a chat with her on Monday morning."

It's thinking fast time again. That's three times.

"Oh no, don't!" I say.

"Why not?" asks Mrs Henton.

"Because Mrs Potts might not want anyone to know that parts of her are missing."

Mrs Henton stands perfectly still and glares at me for a moment. Then she smiles sickeningly. "You know, Andrew," she says, "you're a very thoughtful boy. I'm glad you're Warren's friend. It's so good that I have someone I can *trust* . . ."

"Does that mean we can take out my go-cart?"

Warren has blurted it out before I can stop him.

"Go-cart?" Mrs Henton asks. "What do you want with the go-cart? You know you're not allowed to use it after what happened last time. Your gran's never been to visit us since. It's a wonder she didn't die of fright – sitting her in the back and telling her she was SuperGran. I don't know what you were playing at!"

"But, Mum—"

"No," snaps Mrs Henton, "and that's *final*!"

"Er – actually, Mrs Henton," I say, trying to smile sweetly, "it's not *Warren* who wants the go-cart. It's me. I was wondering if I might borrow it for a day or two?"

"*You*, Andrew?"

"Yes," I say, looking innocently into her eyes. "It would be very kind of you – and I promise not to take my gran out on it, if that's what you're worried about."

"What I'm worried about," she says, "is that you won't use it sensibly . . ."

"Oh, I'll use it sensibly," I say, as I think of the six rabbits.

"Well—"

I can see she's beginning to be swayed. It just needs a little more work.

"And I'll bring it back in one piece," I add.

"All right," she says. "So long as your parents don't mind."

Good old Mrs Henton! Thanks to her, Operation Pedal Paw is one step nearer now.

"Warren," she adds. "Show Andrew where the go-cart is. And you may as well go round to his house, to make sure his mother knows where it's come from."

Warren stares at me in disbelief.

"String," I hiss.

"What?" he asks, too loudly.

"We need some string," I try to whisper. But Mrs Henton has heard me.

"There's enough string on it. You don't need any more."

"So we *are* going to your house?" asks Warren as we trundle along the road, pulling his go-cart behind us.

"'Course we are," I reply.

"I thought we were going to the churchyard . . ."

"We need some string and a large cardboard box first," I tell him.

"What for?" he asks.

"For the rabbits! You don't expect them to sit happily in your go-cart when we pull them along the road, do you?"

"Oh," he answers. He seems to agree with me – but then he stops perfectly still. "Here – I've just thought of something!" He chuckles out loud and it sounds like water running down a plughole. "If they're female rabbits, we could call this a doe-cart, not a go-cart!"

He clutches at his stomach and his shoulders start bobbing up and down. Any minute now, he'll be rolling about on the ground.

"Was that a joke?" I inquire, and I walk off, pulling his go-cart behind me.

He gets the message and is soon walking along at my side again. "Sorry," he says.

I ignore him.

When we reach my house, I leave Warren with the go-cart at the gate and then I tiptoe indoors. It's Saturday afternoon, so I know Dad'll be listening to Sport on Five and Mum'll be round at Aunt Rosie's – probably checking to see I didn't leave my bike there after all.

From the understairs cupboard I take out the large cardboard box that the stereo unit came in, and I know I'll find some string in the kitchen drawer. Then I creep out of the house again, as quietly as I can.

"Shut that door after you!" Suddenly, Dad's voice booms from the lounge – but, luckily, he doesn't come to see what I'm doing.

I rejoin Warren, put the string in the box and the box on the go-cart – and then we make our way at last towards the churchyard.

As we're going along, Mr Higgs and his wife

pass in their car – but they're on the other side of the road and don't notice us.

"Perhaps they're looking for Florence," suggests Warren.

We reach the churchyard.

Clambering over the crumbling brick wall is easy enough. Getting six rabbits out of their cage and into the cardboard box is more difficult.

"Should've brought a carrot," suggests Warren.

"Shut up and hold the box still," I tell him. "Make sure you're keeping it properly over the opening, otherwise they'll all escape – like Florence – and we'll never catch them."

"*Whaaah*!" shouts Warren nervously, as the cardboard box starts wobbling violently.

Success at last! The rabbit with the one black ear has gone from the cage and through, into the open cardboard flaps.

"Hold on!" I cry. "Don't let go of the box!"

Warren looks none too happy – but it's not long before all the other rabbits have been persuaded to join their black-eared friend. However, pushing the flaps shut and getting the box away from the cage proves something of a problem. We very nearly lose a couple of the rabbits, but manage to poke them back just in time. Also, the string won't stay put when I wind it round and round the box.

I wish I'd stayed longer in the Cubs. I should have mastered the tying of knots before I left.

"Well?" says Warren. "Now what?"

I can see what he means.

We manage with some difficulty to lift the wriggling box on to the go-cart, but we still have to get the go-cart back over the brick wall.

"Oh well – here goes," I say and, ramming the go-cart forward, I manage to demolish half a metre of crumbling brickwork. I notice that the rabbit box doesn't look too secure, so I decide we'd better keep our hands on top of it, to stop it bursting open.

"Do you think they'll try to tunnel their way out?" asks Warren.

"It's a cardboard box, not Colditz, you nut," I

tell him – but I watch the sides carefully, just in case.

It's a slow journey, with Warren pulling the string to drag the go-cart along and with me walking at the side, making sure the box stays in its place.

We are just out of the churchyard gate and have turned in the direction of home when Warren stops still in his tracks.

"L-look!" he stammers – and he backs away behind me, still clutching the go-cart string. I look up and, I must say, I feel pretty nervous myself. Walking towards us, just a few metres away, is the man dressed all in black. . . .

"*Run!*" I shout and we turn to run in the direction of Grindley Hill. Even Warren doesn't stop to complain that we're going in the direction of his dentist's again.

To my amazement, I find that the cardboard box, the go-cart and Warren are rapidly moving away from me.

"*Warren!*" I shout – but he doesn't seem to hear me.

I can see why he isn't allowed to take the go-cart out on his own. As we go faster and faster down the hill, so does the cart – and it almost slips from his grasp.

"Hey, hang on a minute!" Warren calls after it. You'd think he was talking to a dog. Most people know that go-carts don't take much notice of spoken instructions. Warren's go-cart is no exception. It continues down the hill, gathering speed, with the box containing the rabbits bouncing up and down like a yo-yo. Instead of helping to stop the cart, passers-by freeze against the walls and watch it rattle by, with Warren and me in hot pursuit.

Before it reaches the bottom of Grindley Hill, I know what's going to happen.

"*Left!*" I yell to Warren. "TURN THE CART TO THE LEFT!"

He doesn't.

The go-cart bounces merrily across the zebra crossing – with luck, not a car in sight – and it keeps on rolling.

The supermarket doors are straight ahead of us, shut fast. As Warren and the go-cart approach, they shoot open as if to welcome them.

I follow a few seconds later and what I see is not a pretty sight.

Warren is sliding in, feet first, through the section that's meant for the trolleys, and the go-cart is heading for the customer's turnstile.

There is a loud *clang* as the cart makes contact with the metal barrier. Then it turns on its side and, as it turns, the string comes undone. The cardboard box falls to the ground and – yes, you've guessed it – the rabbits hop out and make their escape.

It's like Mrs Potts's beads all over again. Trouble

is, these are six rabbits – and they are well and truly alive!

Fortunately, the supermarket doors had shut tight again after Warren, the go-cart and I came crashing in. Therefore, the rabbits' only route of escape is through the store itself. Unfortunately, they seem to know this. Rabbits are smarter than you'd think!

A shop crowded with customers on a Saturday afternoon is not the best place for half a dozen live rabbits to do some exploring. It's amazing how quickly those little creatures can move when they feel the need.

I see that the rabbit with the black ear has already found his way to the frozen food compartments and is busy nibbling at a packet of Brussels sprouts.

By this time, people are beginning to notice.

Some are shouting, a few are screaming and a couple of the store's security men are trying to do a citizen's arrest on whichever rabbit hops into sight.

"Get up, Warren!" I shout. "Scarper – before it's too late!"

I turn to leave – but the entrance doors are still shut fast. In a flash, I realize that my only hope is to go through the shop and out by the exit doors.

I glance at Warren and I can't believe what the idiot's doing. He's chasing after the rabbits!

"Leave them!" I cry, but it's too late . . .

The largest one is going hippity-hop along the top of the meat counter.

61

"I knew they had a good turn-over," an old man says, looking surprised, "but I didn't know their meat was *that* fresh."

By now, the rabbit has hopped happily behind the dairy products and disappeared from sight.

Screams and shouts from different parts of the store tell me where the others have managed to find their way.

I am torn between following Warren round the store or making my exit as fast as I can.

I glance towards the checkouts in time to see one customer about to pack her shopping into a carrier bag when the bag gets up and hops off on its own. She shrieks and faints backwards into a pile of wire baskets. The rabbit hops out of the carrier bag and watches her for a moment, then goes off to join his friends.

"Oh no," I cry as the largest of the rabbits reappears, two checkouts further down. He is on top of the cash till and, in one leap, he manages to land on the head of the blonde cashier.

"Eekk!" she screams. "My hair!"

"No," says Warren, "our rabbit!" He grabs hold of the animal. Unfortunately, he tugs too hard and the lady's blonde wig comes off as well. Her real hair has streaks of red and green in it. I think I like it better than the wig.

Two security men are approaching the checkouts. The shorter one has caught Warren and is
holding him firmly by the shoulders. The taller
one is eyeing me and looking a bit vicious.

"These rabbits belong to you," he snarls.
"Right?"

"'Course not," I reply and, as it happens, I'm
telling the truth.

"Whose are they, then?" asks the other one,
slightly loosening his grip on Warren.

Suddenly, a podgy girl comes running up behind
them, all tearful-like. "They're mine!" she shouts.

The taller guard seems taken aback – and, I must

say, I'm pretty surprised myself.

"Yours? How can they be?"

"I'd know them anywhere. That's Black-Ear, the one over there is Thumper—"

She sure has a knack with names.

"—and there should be four others somewhere . . ." Then she bursts into tears. Black-Ear must have recognized her wailing, for he hops towards her and waits to be stroked.

"Right," says the shorter guard to the podgy girl, "I think you'd better come along with us."

I feel someone tugging at my sleeve.

"Quick – this way. Follow me – while there's a chance!" I look round and I see it's sneery Sandra from school. For once, I'm glad to see her. Somehow she's managed to collect Warren's go-cart and she's brought it to the exit doors.

"Warren!" I hiss – and he stops gawping after the podgy girl who is being led away by the two security guards. We skip out through the exit doors with the go-cart and then drag ourselves up Grindley Hill as fast as we can go. We don't stop until we are sure that no one is chasing after us. Then we puff and blow as hard as we like.

"What were you doing in the supermarket?" I ask Sandra as we move in the direction of the churchyard.

"Following you," she says. "I've been following you all day."

"Don't give me that old tale! What've we been doing?"

"That's what I've wondered," she says, sarcastic-like.

"We're detectives," says Warren, proudly.

"You can't be very good if you didn't know I was behind you! First you had a look at the school playground, then you pinched a bike from the churchyard, took it to Warren's house—" and she goes on to list every blooming thing we've done. "Finally," she says, "you let loose those rabbits you stole from that house . . ."

I must admit, it's a bit of a shock.

"House? What house? It was just a piece of wasteland."

"An overgrown garden, stupid. Didn't you see that there was fencing all round, except for the churchyard wall?"

"Yeah, but—"

"Well, you should've seen there was a doorway as well. That ground's all part of the house – private property – and you've only gone and stolen six rabbits from it!"

"Six? How did you know there were six?" asks Warren.

"The girl who lives there just said so, in the supermarket," Sandra answers smugly. "And you'll never guess who her father is . . ."

"Don't tell me," I gulp. "I think I know . . ."

"He's a police sergeant!" she cries, triumphantly. "So you've really done it now, Marshy Mellows. I wouldn't be surprised if you don't get at least six years – one for each rabbit!"

"Hey," shouts Warren suddenly, "there's Florence!"

"Where?" I ask – and I look in front of me to see Mr Higgs's secret weapon strolling contentedly along the pavement, as if she had never been lost in her life. When she reaches the school gate, she turns and glances back towards us disdainfully, before slinking out of sight.

"I might have known she'd find her own way home," sighs Warren.

VII

As we reach the school gate, we are surprised to see it is standing wide open and that in the playground there is a battered white van, its back doors almost hanging from their hinges. Florence has stopped just beneath the number plate to wash the end of her tail – but when she sees Warren standing gawping at her, she must have memories of what happened last time they met. She stops preening herself and suddenly leaps up inside the open van.

"Oh no, she'll *really* get lost this time!" shouts Warren and he jogs through the gate and into the empty playground.

"What are you doing now?" asks Sandra.

"Getting Florence out of the van, of course," Warren replies – but he doesn't get the chance.

At that moment, the door of the main school building springs open and a guy in white overalls comes out, carrying the box with the word processor in it.

"You leave that van alone, kid," he snaps. "Get right away! What do you think you're doing?"

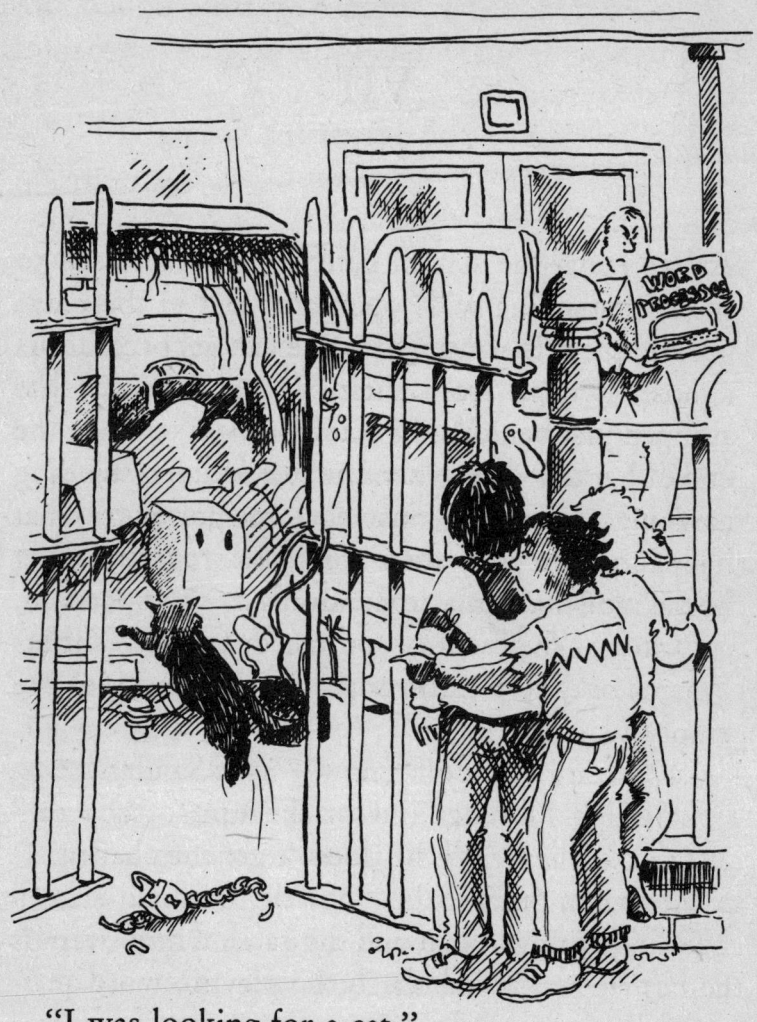

"I was looking for a cat."

"Well, you won't find one in there – just boxes."

"What's wrong, Sid?"

A bearded bloke has appeared at the school door now, struggling under the weight of carrying our two computer boxes.

"Just some boy and his mates nosing around. Nothing to worry about. Go on, get out – or, as soon as I've loaded these boxes, I'll give your ear such a belting . . ."

"Charming!"

Warren backs towards Sandra and me.

"Where are you taking those computers?" Sandra pipes up, bold as brass.

The two men freeze, then after a moment they carry on loading the van as if she hasn't said a thing. The three boxes are dumped roughly into the back of the van and the doors are slammed as tight shut as they will go. Then the bloke with the beard hurries into the driving seat.

"Get in, Sid," he calls. And he starts to rev up the engine. "They were faulty – we're taking them back. You're getting a new lot, right?" says the first guy as he bundles himself into the passenger seat.

Then, before we know it, the van has sped across the tarmac and out through the playground gate.

"Well – we haven't even had a go on those computers yet," moans Warren.

"No – but *they* have. Use your brain," says

Sandra. I wish she wouldn't keep treating us like idiots. "They're not taking them back anywhere this late on a Saturday afternoon – they've nicked them, that's what they've done!"

I have to admit it. I think Sandra's right.

"Nicked 'em?" says Warren in disbelief.

"If not, why would they leave the school door open? And where's Mr Higgs?"

"Perhaps he's inside, waiting to lock up again . . ."

"Don't be daft. He and Mrs Higgs must still be out – their car's not around."

Warren frowns, but then he says, "Poor Florence – why didn't the van men see her?"

"Never mind Florence – what about our computers?" I groan.

"If you're right, Sandra," says Warren, "shouldn't one of us have taken their van number?"

"DCN 364T," answers Sandra. She was always good at figures. "Best thing we can do is try to follow them."

"How are we going to do that?" I sneer. "You can't get up much speed on a go-cart – unless it's all downhill!"

"Right in one. That's where we're making for – Grindley Hill. The van drove off in that direction

– we can go-cart down and hope they keep to the main road as it bends round. With luck, we may see which way they're heading after that, then we can tell the police. Come on!"

"But if the van takes a side turning—"

"Stop nattering!"

I've never moved along a pavement so fast in my life.

The go-cart rattles and creaks and at one point it sounds as if the wheels are about to fall off. They don't, and the three of us arrive again at the top of Grindley Hill.

"Jump in," says Sandra. "I'll steer."

I climb on the back and we leave Warren panting along behind us.

"Hey, hang on! It *is* my go-cart!" he screams.

"Sorry, mate – no room," I shout back at him. "You'll just have to wait for the next one!"

Sandra and I gather speed down the hill. All the pedestrians get out of the way when they see us coming.

The crossing will soon be looming up and I begin to hope that Sandra is better at controlling the go-cart than Warren.

As it happens, she is.

There's quite a disturbance in front of the super-market and all the shoppers have piled out on to the zebra crossing, holding up the traffic. The rabbits have spilled out as well and they are playing "Can't Catch Me" with everyone in sight. Sandra pulls back the string and brings the go-cart neatly to a halt in the centre of the zebra crossing, at the feet of a burly police sergeant.

"It's Podgy's dad," I whisper – and Podgy isn't too far away.

"That's one of them, Dad," she cries, pointing at me, "and there's another!"

I look over my shoulder at Warren, who has just arrived, wheezing after his marathon.

"Right!" says the police sergeant – and he means it. I can tell from his tone of voice that he's not going to stand for any nonsense. "So, you're the ones, are you?"

"No," shouts Sandra. "*They* are!" She points into the traffic jam caused by all the fun and games on the zebra crossing.

"Out of the go-cart!" orders the sergeant.

I take no notice.

"She's right!" cries Warren, bouncing up and down like a yoyo.

"I'm warning you—" continues the sergeant, and his voice sounds even less happy.

"Bull's eye!" I shriek. I've also caught sight of the white battered van, trapped two cars back from where we are.

"They're the ones you should be arresting, Sergeant," Sandra tells the policeman, pointing at the two overalled figures behind the van's windscreen.

"They've stolen our computers!"

"And Mr Higgs' cat!" adds Warren.

"Look – *I'm* concerned about these rabbits . . ."

I can tell the sergeant isn't used to being side-tracked.

Suddenly Sandra makes a dash for the rear of the van and she tugs open the doors.

"There you are!" she says, triumphantly, and Florence jumps out into her arms with a loud miaow.

"Who's that?"

"Florence, the cat I told you about."

"And there – there are the boxes with *our* computers," says Sandra. "Come and look for yourself, Sergeant – please."

"Hang on, now – you can't go breaking into people's vans, young lady," says the van driver, hurrying to close the back doors again.

"What about you breaking into our school?" Sandra accuses him.

"Never been anywhere near your school."

"Then how did Florence get in your van?"

I can see the police sergeant is beginning to take an interest. He forgets about Podgy's rabbits and wanders over to the van.

"Sid's been near our school, haven't you?" Sandra asks the man in the van.

"No I haven't," he replies nervously.

"How did you know this gentleman's name?" asks the sergeant.

"I heard the bearded man say it in the school playground!" Sandra replies.

"These *are* all your computers, are they, sir?" the sergeant asks the driver.

"What's the problem, officer?" Sid asks, dead casual. He's decided to get out of the passenger seat and join his mate.

"No problem, sir. Just wanting confirmation that all these boxes of computers are yours."

By this time, I am round the back of the van myself and I see that there are about a dozen different-shaped boxes piled inside.

"These are our ones," I say, as I spot the three nearest the doors.

"Rubbish!" says the bearded bloke.

"Can you prove it, sir?" asks the sergeant as he casually lifts the lid of the box containing what was meant to be *our* word processor.

Suddenly something falls to the floor of the van and rolls along.

Something small and round and white.

Teeth flash before my eyes.

"Mrs Potts's bead!" I shout, triumphantly. "Here's your proof, Sergeant – this belongs to our

75

school secretary, Mrs Potts." I hold up the bead in triumph before the bewildered look of the van driver, his mate, the police sergeant, Sandra and Warren. "If you search the box, I shouldn't be surprised if you find a lot more." He finds five, to be exact.

"Sergeant, surely you're not going to believe three little kids?" the van driver says, trying it on again. Podgy's dad looks like he does, so the van driver and his mate try to make a run for it. The sergeant whips out his pocket radio for reinforcements, but he needn't have bothered. Suddenly there are enough shoppers surrounding the two crooks to stop them getting further than this side of the zebra crossing.

"Look!" shouts Warren, pointing. Not again, I think. What's he spotted this time? "I thought you said the go-cart was no good without the cardboard box?" Warren says.

It's the podgy girl.

While we've all been busy unmasking the computer thieves, she's been busy calling together all her pet rabbits.

St Francis could have learnt something from her.

The six rabbits are all sitting perfectly still in Warren's go-cart and she's standing beside them, holding the string.

VIII

As it happens, Warren and I get a severe telling off for mistakenly stealing the rabbits. Then we receive a long lecture on the hygiene problems we've caused for the supermarket and the trade they've lost.

Later, it turns out the two men in the van haven't just stolen our school's computers and word processor – they've stolen videos, televisions, computers and word processors from schools and clubs all over the place. They'd have got away with thousands of pounds of equipment if it hadn't been for us. So that's why we get off lightly. No supper and straight to bed.

"Will there be a reward?" I ask on Sunday morning.

Mum just glares.

"Think yourself lucky the supermarket isn't prosecuting us," growls Dad. "You could've cost us a fortune!"

During Sunday evening, there's a ring at the bell. When I open the street door, what do you think

I find?

It's my bike, propped against the gate.

It's got a pink toy rabbit tied to the saddle.

I swear I see the back of Sandra disappearing behind the neighbour's hedge, but I'm so pleased to get my bike back that I decide to give up detective work.

Monday morning is a bit of a let-down.

The local news summary on breakfast TV has a picture of Sandra as the girl who thwarted a series of robberies – nothing at all about Warren or me.

It doesn't seem fair somehow.

When we get to school, we hear that the bike is still missing from the other school – "Things do get stolen, children," says Mrs Brandon – but the five rabbits who went missing from the infant school turned up at the house of one of the kids.

"And now, children," the head says, "I'd like you to welcome a special visitor who is joining our assembly for the first time this morning." I look round and get a real shock.

From the back of the hall comes the man dressed all in black. The only trouble is, he's not wearing a scarf or an overcoat today and he's got a white collar round his neck.

"This is Mr Stanley, the new curate at St Mark's Church," says Mrs Brandon. "Say good morning to Mr Stanley, children."

I suddenly remember the rusty bike that is still hidden among the flower pots in Warren's garden shed.

This afternoon, after school, I decide that Warren and I will be going back to the churchyard to perform a small miracle for the curate – well, we'll be returning his bike, anyway.

Later this morning, Miss Harris expects us to write another story. This time it's got a dead original title: WHAT I DID FOR MY WEEKEND.

"And I expect you all to write at least a page," she says.

I decide I'd prefer to write a story about how our teacher gets gobbled up by a word processor which fancies a byte to eat – and how she is never seen again.

I shouldn't be surprised if I get sent to Mrs Brandon.

Unless, of course, I've managed by then to master that warthog spell . . .